Good Morning, Harry
Good Night, Daddy

Written by **Katy Beebe**

Illustrated by **Valeri Gorbachev**

Eerdmans Books for Young Readers

Grand Rapids, Michigan

In the big-city bustle of London, as the sun sinks down, Daddy heads to work.

"Hullo, Bill!"

Far away, on the sands of Sennen Cove,

Harry and Gran head home for tea.

"Hullo, moggy! Hullo, pups!"

On platform five, Daddy shouts, "All traveling
the London-Penzance sleeper must now be aboard.
All aboard!"

In the snug kitchen of the cottage, Mummy says,
"Supper's ready!"

Harry helps Baby open wide for mushy peas.

Chug–chug–chug.

Here comes the train.

Chug–chug–chug.

Here comes the spoon.

As the London-Penzance sleeper rumbles out of
town, Daddy helps the passengers find their cabins.

"Mind your bags. Cabin three. Tickets please.
All comfy?" asks Daddy.

As the rain patters the windows in the cottage by the sea, Harry, Gran, and Mummy finish a game of cards.

"Go fish!" says Harry.

Whoo-whoo sings the train, rocking on its way.

"Cooo-cooo," says Baby, wishing he could play.

As the London-Penzance sleeper whistles through the countryside, Daddy is hard at work.

"Top berth here, bottom berth there. Lights here, sink there. Anything you need, I'm just down here."

Far away, Harry and Baby are busy too.

"Make sure you wash behind his ears," says Gran.

The wind growls outside the little cottage in
Sennen Cove. Inside, T-Rex bobs up and down.

Whoo-whoo sings the train, rocking on its way.

"Choo-choo," says Baby, and Harry ducks the spray.

In the dining car, Daddy opens his lunch.

"Thanks for the cuppa, Bill."

"No worries, Pete. Cheers."

As the clock in Sennen Cove chimes eight, Harry and Baby get ready for bed.

"Time for a lullaby," says Mummy.

Whoo-whoo sings the train, rocking on its way.

"Too-ra-lee, Too-ra-loo," sings Mummy,
winding down the day.

Early in the morning, Daddy says, "Welcome to Cornwall! Hope you travel with us again. Mind the gap. All depart!"

Early in the morning, Mummy says, "Look who's awake!"

Whoo-whoo sings the train, rocking on its way.

But in the snug little cottage, Harry hears the front door open . . .

"Where're my favorite boys?" says Daddy.

Whoo-whoo sings the train, rolling back to London.

"Tooray-Tooroo!" shouts Harry, bouncing in Daddy's arms.

"Porridge for supper?" asks Mummy.

"Grand!" says Daddy. "Nice way to end the day."

Good morning, Harry.

Good night, Daddy.